Grandfather Twilight

Barbara Berger

PAPERSTAR

The Putnam & Grosset Group

Library of Congress Cataloging-in-Publication Data
Berger, Barbara, Grandfather Twilight.
Summary: At the day's end, Grandfather Twilight
walks in the forest to perform his evening task,
bringing the miracle of night to the world.
[1. Twilight—Fiction.   2. Night—Fiction] I. Title.
PZ7.B4513Gr 1984 [Fic] 83-19490
ISBN 0-698-11394-2
5 7 9 10 8 6

Grandfather
Twilight

To Dad

Grandfather Twilight lives among the trees.

When day is done, he closes his book,
combs his beard, and puts on his jacket.

Next, he opens a wooden chest that is
filled with an endless strand of pearls.
He lifts the strand, takes one pearl from it,
and closes the chest again.

Then, holding the pearl in his hand,
Grandfather Twilight goes for a walk.

The pearl grows larger with every step.

Leaves begin to whisper. Little birds hush.

Gently, he gives the pearl to the silence
above the sea.

Then Grandfather Twilight

goes home again.

He gets ready for bed.

And he goes to sleep.

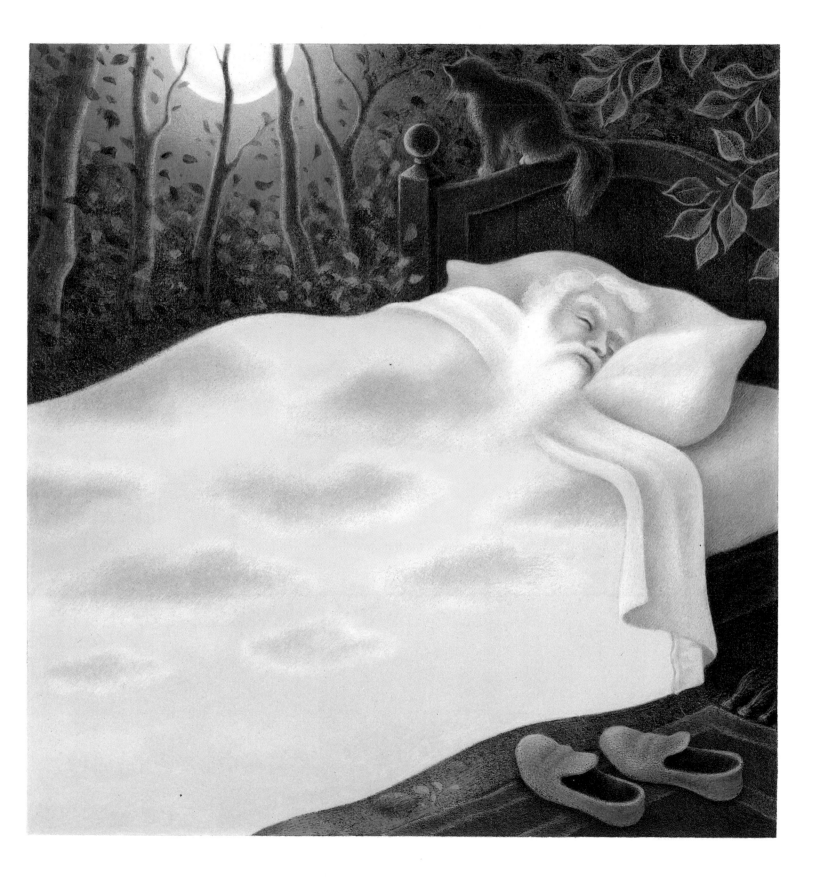

Good night.